LOS
THE PLOT

'*Losing the Plot* . . . is earthed in love, curiosity, and interlinked story of mother and son, Twi & English, Owusu takes risks with a joy that makes his prose soar . . . an inimitable talent' JENNI FAGAN

'[Owusu] bares his soul in such an auspicious manner, you're immediately transported into his world and he dares you to feel what he feels' ELIJAH LAWAL

'Owusu is one of the most original writers today' STEFAN TOBLER

'A densely poetic act of resistance' *Times Literary Supplement*

'A beautiful portrayal of a child recognising the vulnerability of their parent' *New Statesman*

'A polyphone of voices, cadences and styles' *Scotsman*

'Owusu's writing is bold, wise and generous; he amplifies and validates the complexities of inter-generational love' *British Blacklist*

'A novel that pierces you right in the heart' *Face*

Also by Derek Owusu

That Reminds Me
Safe: On Black British Men Reclaiming Space (ed.)
About This Boy: Growing Up, Making Mistakes and
Becoming Me (with Leon Rolle)

LOSING THE PLOT

DEREK OWUSU

CANONGATE

This paperback edition first published in Great Britain in 2023
by Canongate Books

First published in Great Britain, the USA and Canada in 2022
by Canongate Books Ltd, 14 High Street, Edinburgh EH1 1TE

canongate.co.uk

1

British Library Cataloguing-in-Publication Data
A catalogue record for this book is available on
request from the British Library

ISBN 978 1 83885 564 2

Typeset in Bembo by
Palimpsest Book Production Ltd, Falkirk, Stirlingshire

Printed and bound in Great Britain by Clays Ltd, Elcograf S.p.A.

For our mothers. For our aunties.
And, of course, for Berthy.

LANDING

I

The plane breaks through grey squalls, directionless to all but the small girl feeling the craft balance before it blooms through moist shrooms leaving a country in its second childhood for another promising the same to her, the girl, whose head is shaven by the attention of fingers like soldiers instructed to dictate how low. She reaches up and rubs a hand over what survived at the roots, too unnerved in her hometown to curl around the toll and contrast of time, but perhaps new land will lay new ground.

Her return will be buried in the humid and dusty trails of Jamasi, beneath potholes and shallow thoughts, where Auntie put her into a cab barely pieced together – orange puzzle pieces displaying an imbalance with parts and paths – with two small plastic bags full of water, another dripping fried rice in her trouser pocket and a backpack containing a few items of clothing, some paperwork. And a passport.

She'd only seen two photos of herself – the first, fallen, retreating to the dust, was snatched from her hands and encased in the pages of a bible, the second, inside another book, but green, her embellishing face held in place by plastic, material finally, protected by the highlighted Republic of Ghana.

Importance impresses on every item as she gathers her thoughts, telling herself again who to look for, the age she is supposed to be and which date carries her birthday – details that will fall when a lowered head faces British breeze because who cares how long or when, so long as she's there.

To her right, she fights not to be consumed by the compulsion to look, losing so many times the obronis sitting in the next aisle of broken seats may assume she's inviting them over, those twisting and polishing her tongue,* blowing grammar without savouring the sound, a switched tempo, contorted into another language.

Do her sisters know she has gone? She pauses to touch on a framed life in reverse, a wonder as splashes of Technicolor appear.

She was sent away, told Auntie would watch her from now, because the house was too small and she was the eldest, she'd had more life with family, her arguments not allowed to conclude even though when she lands, new documents will read her younger than every sibling.

But anyway it's fine. Because Akos – Akos, her auntie, one who may have only seen clean terrazzo or splintering brown arms too weak to pound or fold, just one to return glass that once contained orange juice made sweeter with stolen sips, Akos – Akos knew what this small girl was meant for. It was she who arranged the flight, knew where to go for Foreign Affairs and waved palm fronds as she chased the taxi, panting in Twi or Fante – *remember where*

* Okay, so do I just start speaking? Alright cool. Yeah, don't worry, I got one. Aight, one time we were en route somewhere in Tottenham. My mum bumped into some old friend in the back of the bus. They raise their voices, doing all of that, eiiis and phrases in Twi. Some bald guy in front of us, head shiny like ivory or something, glistening, but I deeped it start turning red, bare patches – man was frustrated. He kept turning around until my mum's friend, Auntie, everyone is an auntie, really, flicked her nose up to him and said something, can't even remember what. I thought she recognised him. My mum, who also moved like she knew him, said his name: 'Who? Obroni?'

you came from, words built upon or containing *I can get by without you.*

Or sadness.

Perhaps sadness.

The girl looks out the window and wonders which cloud holds the weight of Awurade.* This is His home, giving her way to pass unscathed, one body of water to another, disturbing His lathered sky, but for her He doesn't mind. My daughter, it is fine. *Yes, God is guiding this plane,* she thinks. *God will lead me through.*

Eii, aburokyire† – a new life looms as single thread weaves through the corner of her cheek, pulling the beginnings of a smile as the thought lands.

* My mum used to pray for hours. Whenever I'd get bored, I'd go into her room and watch her walking about, moving absolutely mad and punching up the air, calling out bare different names. But they all meant the same thing. Trust me, it was the same spirit. Or something like it.

† And she loved to act like she didn't care for Ghana, or even the Ghanaians who were here in ends. But anytime she was on the phone, and they'd say something about a schoolmate or something like that, suddenly she was interested, asking when they got here, where they're staying, soo excited, even though I know she loved to think England was only her thing. And yet always worrying about next people and their business. I wish I could kiss my teeth and people could hear it.

II

I have come from the cornershop and now I must cook too. Ei, making life. I'll keep the coppers until he asks. Oh, mi were firi,* I'll tell him, how can I steal? Wofaa,† he sweats while he eats. Who can adjust to this cold, so his tongue asks for more mako,‡ even too much, his mouth smelling when we sleep. Me, I turn away but he wakes and he tells me to look at him, look at this man, is this looking after me? He thinks he's doing me; I will hold my breath until God delivers and judges his filty turumu. §

But . . .

Should I try and wash him in the night.

I should say I added more pepper when I didn't.

I should find work.

*Listen, now that I'm older, my memory is gone, dead – I go to shop for one thing, and come back with something completely different. Now I can see how my mum felt.

† When it comes to Ghanaian culture, most man older than you, maybe like ten years older. You know what, maybe even less sometimes, you have to call them uncle. Blood or not, hate them or not, still gotta respect them man. Like, I know most the people reading the book, I'd have to call them uncle or auntie, get me?

‡ But you see them older Ghanaians, they'll always cook for you, or the man will shout for their wife to make something, drop one, two eggs on the corn beef stew with rice, even if they just met you. My mum was like that, still. One thing I really miss about my mum's cooking is how she could balance spices and pepper perfectly without cancelling out the heat or flavours.

§ But those kinda spices stick to you, fingers smelling like soup the next day if you don't wash properly. When I was a yout, I hated taking baths. But my mum would say she could smell my bum. And I get self-conscious. Fam. You're laughing but I'm not joking. Did anyone even teach me how to wipe my bum? Had to learn that myself.

7

Leave.

He won't like it.

But can he strike me before God will strike him?

My coins will drop to him, anyway.

Awurade, London is doing me rough.

*Adwuma nyε easy.**

Anyway, let me leave him.

I'll stay inside till he comes back.

Collect some pessoas when I collect his beer.

Collect some spit to spice his nkwan.

Then he can sleep, and who knows if I will run.

Aboa.†

* She weren't even clean herself. And she had about three cleaning jobs, fam. I never noticed before how hard she was working. And how that shit was breaking her down. Got a job as soon as she landed, basically, so was always stressed and stressing me. Every day complaining about her back, like telling me about it just before I'd ask her for something.

† And every day insulting man when she don't get what she wants. Sometimes it's jokes, though, can't lie, like how you call someone a dickhead with that cheeky grin on your face. But back in the day I know she weren't really smiling like that so it was probably hard to tell when she was running joke with her insults.

III

Time collapses as the value rises, bossman turning away complaints, a fifty pence scratching through the code, quickly becomes a ten pence dragged across the numbers that disclose.

A day becomes every other and weekly silences quiet her enthusiasm for home. They are too busy, she thinks, but it's her, she's the one who is here.

The distance between death and life proclaims absences unbearable. Distant glimpses of waning villages assuage the emotions of scarcity.

She stops calling and spends more time
with her brood of thoughts; she finds extra
shifts to take her mind off what she's lost.

IV

For those who just come, packs only just open, the world, Tottenham, is a village of disguised loan shops adjacent to Ladbrokes and William Hill bookmakers,

the former having the latter's back, of course,

with a few slightly slanted juiced-upped stores,

the voice flogging fruit next door needing only to look up from his stall to see how easily he could be crushed.

A miasma filled with beeping bus doors interrupting the reveries of those who now begin to run,

hoping the driver is having a good morning without tricksters getting on expecting change for ten-pound notes,

used Vespas chopping through the roads,
a pulling of a chord splitting the air when
a rev rolls a wrist,
    punks turn round,
    gelled hair trapping sound,
side streets propelling residents to
chopped shops for meats, fish, Maggi and
magnesia, but an incomplete journey until
a tête-à-tête with a face as singular as hers.

V

She takes her place in front of the church,
looks up to the ascending seats and out
the rear windows.

She is singing for Awurade, though when
she walks along golden streets her lowered
eyes smoulder; the light seen can suddenly
pull the rigid pieces of a heart back
together, seamless, make you miss,
remember, the only thing that truly matters.
Yesu, Lord and Saviour.

The pastor raises his hand and she begins.
Her voice is not perfect but she comes as
she is to praise, every missed note or incor-
rect tone affirming the shared reach for a
measure of goodness.

She croons the chorus, still no inspiriting from the church; had she the desire to face them, she'd notice deliberate fidgeting and hands in laps raising slightly to cast her away. But she sings on – a break in her voice, a crack snaking through the melody, roof splitting, the sky separating to inspire her downpour.

The second chorus is softer but, still, her songs of praise cannot be held without scouring the hands that try. No one in the hall is willing to extend themselves, screwing up their faces because this young woman has stolen time, would have absconded with their sympathy, even pity would satisfy this one.

They know. She holds the final note while lowering her head. Finally, she sees and knows no matter where she goes, she will be surrounded by distance, every place she settles a different version of the same thing.

But it's okay. She is filled for now, the cold aerated hall condensing each breath, the heavy clouds above her an inert creation, sung to life to wait for death. But it's okay, she wipes her eyes and goes back to her seat, hope now holding up her frame, making her impervious to floating disdain, a God's glance supposed to uplift, bypass a side-eye peering from a plane heaving with expectations. But still, she hums the song to herself. Made in His image. Speaking to God without moving her lips.

VI

Pages of her New Testament will remain in Twi,

But she hopes truth will strip a griot's tongue.

The tithe took its toll, envelopes unfold,

They know the word of God will never be free.

She pushes through, dragging chairs for new renditions,

The notes will maintain the church,

But from her pocket she passes coins to make up four,

So supplier, anointed, sprays, dampening her with shame – it's better you find more cleaning! – a good book withheld from poor impurity.

Oh, her whisper –

Dropped coin, a dropped head, she touches the fallen bronze, kneeling, shoes sliding dust into her mouth.

A cough – a life ceremoniously swallowed – to say, what He maketh from dust will soon decay.

So her beat-up words will have to do, but as long as she believes,

The brass coin will still feed her a week from now, so with all that, she quietly leaves.

VII

She had lingered, passing over duty to dismiss dust with liquid and rag.

And then she called to him, a shy diffusing laugh, a siren's balmy murmur wearing down his wax.

The chosen colleague rubbed the panes he often used to glance behind, meant for students wondering when they could play outside.

But with his turn, all he saw was her steps towards the door, awkward hips, prolonging and stiff, a moment meant to imprint, blocked.

The vacuum, another morning cleaner jammed by the door, waiting for her touch, happy to be there, waiting to be pulled away.

* So, apparently, I don't look Ghanaian. My mum used to say that all the time. That I look Carib or something. Never Nigerian, though. But to be honest, those man are getting it in so it wouldn't even be an issue. But I can't lie, I've never really understood what it means when people say it, but I kinda get where they're going with it, one nation and that. You look Ghanaian. Nah, the one writing notes.

† When people do clock I'm Ghanaian it's always the same questions. Listen, try asks someone to teach you a word in their language, I bet any money the first word they try and teach you is either a swear word or 'hello/how are you'. Yeah, I do that too, can't lie, sometimes it's funny, especially if you say the word means something different. Obviously, my mum didn't start with a bad word when she tried to teach me. Didn't last long, though. Moretime I just learnt everything she'd shout at me. And in the beginning that was the most Twi she'd use anyhow. I guess she was going through it when my dad walked out. Guessing, though.

‡ I remember the response she taught me for 'how are you', was the way she'd reply to it. Like my aunties and that. I heard my dad answer once. And the way he dropped it was so much cooler, so man took that, used it all the time, and I know my mum was pissed.

Pulled –

His eyes can't be. 'Eii asɛm,' he says through a smile that swallows his lips, 'hm, Ghana fuo.'* He twists the volume on his radio.

But today, it's him loitering without work, each frame half caught in the reflection of the spotless tables competing triumphantly with the usual vertical mirroring surfaces.

'Hello, ma,' he says.
   Bra Kwame. Ete sɛn?†
   'Oh, Bɔkɔɔ. We yɛ okay?'‡
   Mmm. Yɛ da Nyame ase.§

* * *

At home, the pestle beats the wooden handle, forcing the tip of the knife into the outside metal ring of evaporated milk. The bent steel widens the cavity. She pours the cream over her cornflakes, adds warm water and stirs.

Sounds out of Broadwater Farm's Ghana station rise in and out of static – presenting voices pirouetting around her flat, graceful through the fragrant door, inviting and interlacing with the dampness and the pepper soup freed from clinging to the walls – taking root as she slows her chewing or spits out flakes at the nonsense of callers.

Eii, asɛm.★ The topic – time of marriage, a topic so cold to her and unkindled that her metronome stood still, sundial lay in darkness, all frozen wheels patient. Yey! She needs to defrost the akrante,† she remembers, puts the bowl down between her crossed legs, opens them, stands and walks to the freezer. Rushing back to the living room she hears the front door close, but the greeting floats in without a volley, because, again, she feels the flourishing she will forever try to subdue, rising and twisting to a laugh that spreads across her face, as again the caller repeats his entreaty – shouting her name and workplace, he tells her to stop this silliness and marry him. *Eii, asɛm.*

§ My mum never really showed it when was vex. But I could always tell when she was. But she thanked God – Awrade or Nyame – for all things, everything, even for me being willing to learn Twi, but that only happened sometimes. To be honest, mostly she ignored me asking or asked me am I living in Ghana that I want to learn Twi.

★ I see why Ghanaians are always thanking God, though, because everything is an exclamation, everything is a problem for them. Everything is suffering; everyone is tired – 'Yesu, ma bre oooo.' I said that once when I was like seven or eight and the way my mum knocked my head and told me to stop my nkwasia sem.

† But it's true, even I was suffering back then. But listen, when you're young, you'll eat whatever. But after a while you start to clock like, rah, what even is this? Sometimes, though, usually as you get older, you realise you have to allow thinking about it and just eat it – if my dad can chop them big pieces of meat, why can't I? You know it ain't beef or chicken but you just have to firm it.

VIII

So you like him? someone asked, assumed,
assigned.

    Yes, why not. He's fine.

    So you had sex?

    Imagine! . . . those wondering pupils
sensing light, withdrawing, so slight. *Yes,*
she spits from a brux clench, *we had se(s)x.
But this is your last. Don't ask me again.*

    So you love him?

    Hmm, you know how we say this in Twi?

    How?

    *Medɔ wo, that's it, but it's him who must
say it to me.*

IX

She could free her fingers through what now grew from her roots – though stunted – and she often thought of what she'd lost to Jerry John, where did these thoughts belong? But touched her cheekbones gratefully, one highlight after the coup d'état, the following famine readying her for abrokekye. No obstacle to her hands down her hips, no violence towards her lips, nostrils closer too, almost like touching fingertips. The English cold and sharp tongues had reshaped a brittle body.

London accentuated all this, the city was an opportunity, bursting with used clothes and jeans that needed less care, and everything borrowed suiting her time, after some weeks she could use her hands –

rubbing together, colouring the warm water with blue and brown, brown and blue.

The tall city buildings enclosing her, a refocus to flats, a teasing reach to the sky for those who live within its walls, but a complement to her stature as she looks up from where she stands. Her smile, envious of gaps but yes, the beauty here will let her in – she's almost used to all these things. Blissful cheeks, she's pleased, still rounded, *I chop more but have eaten less*, large cherries at their peaks, a colour visible on fairer skin in this cold, assumed tolerance if she's unable to blush.

Some want to please only the eyes, dark irises still unlit under any blue sky, but her glasses keep her safe and stylish – she may be disappointed by her position in the world but happy to twirl for her mirrored image.

X

Naive faith in her innocence forces her to
split a chewing stick.

A cold lemon cut open and applied, a
hair picked from the rim before it is tossed.

He watches her and asks what village
she's from in Ghana –

A question that falls from those who
will never land.

XI

But she came and went, danced on his
fingertips. Girth declined with nowhere
else left to climb, but then wealth and
weight gathered again to impress her.
'Contracts' sustained the body for so long
but once scrapped, another scheme set in
motion, something bright behind his head,
Jheri slowly dipping, dripping, so here he
is again, at her door with a bag full of
spiced turkey tail and shito on the side.
She hasn't eaten in days and so takes him
inside.

XII

She tries to translate idioms and sayings
– words placed by how they're spoken as
opposed to their expression.

Conversing silhouettes, filled with mixed
emotions tapping her own, she stands in
their circle, coloured by those speaking.

No, there were no backyards with poultry
begging to be pardoned, padin? No, she'd
never seen anything plucked while she
perspired, cried for a feathered friend, sia,
but anyway, why not?

So, was her culture already distant when
she wished to shun the son on her back?
Do these obronis, no no, colleagues, know

more, intimating a short stay and tilting their heads to a place she could never go back to?

I never stayed in such places, that's not in our culture, you know, we Ashantis . . . Brown dust touches the air as she trails off – though there's no bruising to rise and fall from these questions, she knows there's a warm sting to come from the tongues that convey them.

XIII

With so many seated below, the driver
failing to coerce more above, she climbs
the stairs, thinking back and wondering if
she missed one of her classrooms. She
smells her fingers and pulls back from the
stewed bleach as she walks to the middle
of the upper deck, puts her hands in her
coat pockets and sits. One of the school-
boys tells his friend to turn the music
down, a compromise between filial, no,
cultural, respect and sharing his sick taste
in music; lowering it even further when
something foul approaches. She turns to
the side, just enough, a display to show
she's looking over her shoulder without
doing so, a smile in a lowering head. The
lyrics still surge towards her, tempered,

shouting a whisper hoping to be heard. She hears, dries up inside and breathes a little heavier – a single line smothers chorus and verse, beat dropping to nothing. She takes her hands out of her pockets and looks at them, the lines, the blood and thickness of her fingers. She clenches and then releases, letting the blood find its way back to the centre. She's never done this before, never feared pale hands or understood the indifference at seeing them clasp something and feeling nothing; thinking, as the words still boom and undulate through the wrinkles of matter, grey. Words repeat again and again . . . she thinks, thinks she feels, rubbing her palm along her neck, when will it stop, when will it end . . .

XIV

Who are these men seated behind me? And the account holder, where is he? No, everything is fine, it's okay, I should be still. But eii, me yemu hyɛ hyɛ me.*

As for me, saa Catholicism en yɛ mi denomination,† *so no wine offering, beer? Even that one I denounce it.*

I can't collect his name but my son will arrive into this last, I'm thinking, but I will divorce this man soon because how can this obroni take me, it's me that he loves? It's no way.

By the grace of God mi krataa be ba,‡ *there's no guarantee, but for this child, so he can sleep*

* So there were a lot of things that made my mum nervous: random knocks on the door, random phone calls, parties or funerals she'd forgotten. Watch, she'd hold her stomach like this, rubbing it like say she wants to burp, then next thing you find her walking out of a toilet. Hear her, 'What's your problem?' trying to hold eye contact so it's not awkward. Ah, allow it, man.

† Even in church she was nervous like this. You know what, I never knew how many different types of church there were. And how strict those lot were with their own people. They didn't really mix. Well, that's what it looked like to me. All reading from the same book but screwing up their face at different typa wortship.

‡ My mum has been in the UK for over thirty years and she still struggles to see herself as British, the way she sees it always changes from one day to the next but she has no problem telling me I'm not Ghanaian. She became a citizen before I was even born, been married twice to 'Englishmen', probably just British citizens to be honest, and has lived here longer than me, and yet . . . I know you see what I'm saying.

35

well and me too I can rest, for this handsome boy.

You may **** the ****. And congratulations.

XV

Her bedsheet floats over the pull-out drawer. She feels like a living dawn, facing the world she hopes to return to, remind her of the glory that she once felt radiate. Where is it? She searches — flips the bedsheet onto itself, a tongue reaching for a septum, nervous gestures, dark nights having intimidated, thrown an ominous glow on everything in her room, coerced to conceal paths to any contentment — and pulls out bags she hopes will threaten her reflective pauses.

This one, two pockets to the side put a hold on swift hands, she enjoys,

a melting of circadian rhythm.

The sparse pattern on the next, soothed,

adinkra, incipient.

Another could fit here, lodged beneath her armpit – not too long, stylish, unlike the one with a tall strap, the purse brushing her thigh but still she could hold her hand on the top and do styles.

How close to real does not concern her, a proximate to material is enough to relax then rouse her to life, feel acceptance in a world of labels and tags, chain straps, à la carte, envelope, clutch or baguette, anything to hold the accumulated weight from years that have never offered to cradle her progress.

Faith that her daughter to be brought forth will love this new touch, magnetic clicks falling short of a surprise, her child will know what to expect – yes, she will continue to fashion herself to help give her bodam* grace – the obstacle of items will slow down this impediment's pace.

* There was one time when I tried to convince my mum that she had depression, I think I was like fifteen or something. She was like, yeah, sometimes she's sad, but she never really clocked that I was trying to say it's a mental thing and not an emotional one. When she finally got me, she was like, 'What are you trying to say?' See? Impossible.

XVI

She lifts her head, towel for tresses, watches
as snakes of steam dance and fight to rise
and fall,
    condensing, dripping, drops dying and
spreading,
    reminding her tears cling to the face to
live a little longer.
    She brushes her teeth out of time with
her reflection,
    watches suds touch the porcelain
prefering the scrub and ease of a chewing
stick.

Just a lid of Dettol,
    small small,
    into a bucket bath to heal,

but the last cup of water before the final pour

is no longer diluted, useless, as the damp takes shape on her face.

Her throat is slick, no sweat but delirium.

Nose flares with dry clusters, a mind without the swell.

Static, watching, foundations thud down from the TV screen, something just bought, reshaping her line of sight.

A nice place she lives in she thinks,

the toilet seat no longer loose,

the carpet's thinning hair, restored.

She tries lemon and ginger,

warms soup and watches the spoon spark.

Angel cream on her chest,

rub under breast under ageing duress to dissipate the throb that somehow was left.

Why does she struggle to rise, dread the dregs down her thigh,

Redeemer, what is this, please, a plea, an ask: why?

Chalewote dragged to the kitchen again as with

hot water she adds sliced garlic to her flask.

DISEMBARKING

I

Things have become more still,
    sudden, no distance to be covered.
    No one brushes past.
    They cross roads and can't see.
    Or ask.
    How far?
    Watching without motion, distinguishes
families, grandmother and daughter side
by side,
    until the toddler strolls ahead and the
mother moves out of step.
    What fear touched and flushed her feet
she thinks as she peers from stone, grainy
with the graphite of London.
    Soles have darkened, famished and
embarrassed at how they're worn,

how neglected is the entire body, how separated things have become.

She has a home somewhere she'll need to scour when the sun succumbs,
unbearable is the weight of the sky.

Eventually, yes, thank you, she can focus her eyes, and warm her stomach with the palm of her hand.

II

Once, a pastor preached, a fearless reach
inside the mouth of a beast, words repeat,
the pastor preached, a lion starved and
intimidated by the presence of a will
unbound by the rules of the bush. A thrust
at its throat, a tight fist squeezed saliva from
its tongue before pulling it with the force
of a backslide, the howl let out enlivening
the weak and the meek, the pastor, mouth
wide, he preached.

This fatiguing note fading, departing, a
woman's voice rising, staying, an aspiring
seraph peering down, toes teasing the
church floor, shaming,
    trying to trace further words into the
air with gestures as viscous as her tongue.

She, our mother, peered into this mouth and recalled the story, looking above, ears adjusting, patient,

to catch the possible pitch of a scream when this homily forcefully comes to an end.

No, not me, there will be no blood for this church lion to lick up and savour, she thought, her son will be born even if rejected by the pride.

Her singing chains displayed restraint; grounded, she turned and walked away.

Behind her, this saint's lips still parted, thinking of their own praise,

sanctimonious outrage, the stench of a failed slaughter still assaulting the prey once she's out of the building, looking down the street, waiting, for the bus that will carry her home.

III

She carries her shoes by her side, tarnishing her jeans instead of the walkway, her toes scrunching over the smoothness of the flayed door-to-door carpet sale, touched by iron-like footsteps, pressing clothes on the floor banned from then on, her having to contribute to the bill for damages, landlord unmoved by the creases that adorn her daily. She rents a room for her Bible and Rich Teas, cup, PG Tips, sugar and milk. She stirred once but steel against porcelain woke too many in the house so in the morning, after she apologised, she wrapped it up and dropped it down the chute. She now enjoys the routine lick of her finger. As she passes, gently, hands go up in response to her greeting, if only to show skin. She's thin with stretching herself – emaciated to those who share her space, who stare at foreign flies braving black faces, swarming ads with tears timed to a thirsty cameraman. But for her, they do not move. Pregnancy the revelation once eyes open to the lordosis touching her back, back, that's all anyone gives. She pulls herself up the banister, the spared carpet bristles tickling through the holes in her tights, black polka dots, up and around her legs, thighs that know one thing comes after the other, never expecting to be carried, forever in motion. Before the final step she stops, *aych, ma bre,*★ anyway, she pulls through again, waddles, hand circling her stomach, towards her ajar bedroom door. There are no biscuits left. She sits and stares down at the crumpled packet, hand on her stomach again, she whispers, *Son, kafra, why?*

★ My mum never really complained. She could of, though, like, she has reason to. Always doing something, going somewhere, holding herself back and sometimes even chatting to herself. This woman would never rest. Only between one cleaning job and another and that ain't really rest. Just like waiting in a lobby or something with tea and digestive biscuits.

IV

She supports his body with her crook.
There he sits on her hip as she bends over,
lifting a bottle from her bag, cold, an early
pump for the swelling walnut. She sucks
and draws her tongue back from her own
bitterness.

She continues to plead, bouncing her child
as he mimics speech, contorting his lips
for the tip of the teat.

His mother settles, gathered, shallow pools
on the back of her palms, listening to the
voice before her, shielded by plastic, danger
of the working poor; and the boy now
sucks through his desire diluted by tears

of joy allayed by relief, mother and son
able to rest their heads, together once more.

V

She thought she'd expelled it all, but can't bear to see him when he's awake so averts her eyes until able to cover him when he rests, holds his nostrils closed for ten seconds until he squirms like something stole his breath in his approaching ephialtes, maybe she'll do it again for eleven seconds and if she can hold on a little longer she won't have to send him 'back home', to those expectant, those who see only a child. Twenty seconds before he cries out, feral, this thing from her. *Abonsam,** she pushes through flat-lined lips. She must, she has to hold his nose again, a second more until she can lift him from his cot and sit him on her hip, handled on another brink,

* Sometimes, before my mum came into my room to put me to bed, I remember getting excited about which story she is going to tell me, and the stress that crept up on me too. Anansi was calm, I'd always fall asleep before the end, though. But there were other stories that would wake me up, like, I'd be more awake then than I was in the morning. People like Maame Wata and witch doctors and that. I don't know why lessons of good and bad needed to scare man before I learnt wagwan. I wasn't even that bad. But anyway, like I said, I liked those Anansi stories.

snatch curdled milk from the table, playfully bouncing him to the kitchen to begin boiling water.

VI

She holds and stretches her skin to see the
hiding slick and sparkle of youth untouched
by the childishness of ageing, so fast it
seemed for her.

She has to let it go.

VII

She tightens and folds the ntoma under
her arm
   while eyes from an incepting mind float
around the banks of London,
   resting between the respite of touching
blades, bones,
   weightless, she walks without pause,
without her lord – a circlet fades in and
out on her child's temple.
   She converses about the shops, what's
inside and what she'd like,
   with much reflecting as they walk,
   hoping her baby will recall and when
he grows will then decide.
   His eyes, buoyed or wide, her voice now
has somewhere to reside.

VIII

She has called for one of them, scattered
family sent for the rest, everything coming
together in the first place she's enjoyed
occupying alone, though no time to settle,
constantly handing over keys being the
motive of her life.

Family can become a painful rumour if
the whispers stretch far enough, and with
her family's path converging, all she
imagines is how they'll respond when asked
to remove their shoes.

Everyone sits with hands in laps, one hand
consoling the other after being shaken by
a stranger, though stranger still in Jamasi
or this renamed living quarter in Britain.

We often fail to count the years when a passage loses meaning, we glide our eyes over it knowing there is nothing to redeem the end.

She is polite, serves tea in cracked porcelain, a few bubbles on the surface so asked to clean more thoroughly. *Aren't you a cleaner?* A return with no respect – no longer second to her silhouette, she places cups on the centre table, sour dark brown spilling – she needs to cut down on sweetness, says her GP – throwing work-bonus plastic pots of milk onto their saucers – *dilute if you like, rise if you like!* Or leave with a taste in your throat that will not be quenched in this flat. Can you imagine?

IX

Does she know the texture of a mother?

Once, upon her arrival, she embraced a sister – chins resting on shoulders and bodies pushed back, a West African type of affection that now feels like tender scraps.

Did she hold her auntie before she departed?

Will she hold her son like he was hollow inside, rub down the piloerection when a plane flies above her eyes.

The binding piece shrivels, though she returns to it every day; she'll mother every piece of him, even if parts must be taken away.

Will she stroll through another childhood with dusty and deserting feet.

Will she cry when hands reach, will she let her son suffer her defeat.

IX

X

She walks to give charity
in the land of gold.

Material in suitcases and plastic-wrapped
rectangle tins fill a bottom drawer, many
with the key to turning things around
fallen away.

She recalls the items she begged for
patience, only having set eyes on them
once, turning away from a closed cupboard
or clipped Samsonite, so sure of their flight,
but no concern for knowing when. Every
toaster or kettle kept boxed beneath her
bed, connected and speaking, her obliga-
tions — what she wouldn't allow to be dead.

She wonders if other vessels, concealing
the same guilt, hope to carry gold home
too; one day, one day it will come.

Or is it only she who cares, with a seeded
garden where her machete evolved to
shears: a ribbon in two parts before home.

A family extends, and a path always
bends . . .

She doesn't know, doesn't even know it
makes no difference what she gives, she
can't see to their ends.

She walks to give charity
in the land of gold.

XI

It was supposed to go down easy. An anointed handkerchief spiriting a thumb wipes her son's lips.

An appetite for more separates two fingers before they press into the white mass,

The soup scalds her cuticles as it drips and helps slide the overcast from her finger-tips, large, free, difficult to swallow,

With fear of wastage he pushes his head forward, a straining stretch as he struggles to get it down.

She watches,
  Patient somewhere,
  Silent,
  The strains, white noise to dreamy eyes.

Fufu, laguna full, pounded,

Her thumb delivers another helping over her fingers,

Too soft to choke, but painful.

She watches

Without admission,

Senses,

A hand up to halt his toil, with the chorus, *Hey hey! If it's too big don't try to swallow!*

XII

His hair – just short enough to avoid the comb. He wears ironed corduroy trousers, M&S shirt tucked into his belt with knife notches to keep it tight, shoes that won't bend but shine to compete with freighted areas of Vaseline highlighting poor hands that are never smooth. She watches him, dissatisfied at her lack of material, a shadowy artist detached from their creation, only concerned with perfect iterations, never children.

They step out of the lift and can hear the running around behind the third door down so he pulls his hand out of hers to scratch his head, examining oily scalp collected under his fingernails. 'So you didn't cut your nail!?' she asks, grabs his hand and pulls him forward. 'You want to disgrace me.' Should he? Without knowing the right response, he searches for an answer in what swells inside him every time he's asked a question requiring sight he hasn't yet honed. As always, he says nothing. They get to the door.

There's no run to knocks though the young inside flick the latch up and down – a voice says move from the door – those inside used to the enforcing fists of faceless TV checks. Who is it? Comes a voice. Ɛyɛ me ara, she says back. Voices shushed, giggles suppressed and again her son knocks on the door, with no reply or echo pulled from the silence, onset of confusion and fearful looks from one friend to the other bringing shadows of doubt to life. Her son bends and peers through the letterbox, shouting the name of the birthday boy – though today he is Ernest instead of Kwaku, so an absence of a response is forgivable? He calls Kwaks this time, but in response, a presence – older, wiser, matronly – sensed behind the door. The body behind the door kneels to look through the open flap, figures her lips, rises a little and spits.

Her son steps back as she vaults forward. '*Herh! Wo yɛ kwasia*★ *wo mame twɛ, why*!† *Open this door, you this foolish woman.*' Her son is still wiping his face, still able to smell the odour around his nose as if it continued to fall to his lips. He looks at his mother as she kicks the door, slaps it, screams in a tone he thought only he owned. She summons phlegm and leaves it on the door, walks over to him, saying, pleading. '*Sorry, me yɛ sorry, Kwesi, please, sorry why? Don't mind them. They are stupid. Come, come here, let me look at your face, is it all gone?*'

★ Honestly, certain insults can't even be translated and put into context that makes sense, you just have to feel the vim of the insult and know it's devastating and it's all gonna end with a scrap. Bro, I know this because I've seen it with my own eyes. She's bare small so I didn't even clock she can fight. Like a proper fight not just giving me licks when she was pissed off. Sometimes I think she likes it because the way she used to step to me when I was older, puffing up her small chest, trying to chat like me, telling me 'come den.' Fucking joker. Of course I never had a fight with my mum. C'mon, man, what kinda question?

† There's been a lot of times that my mum has been pushed to the limit, like, to the point where I was even telling her she needs to stop, or I'm telling the other person they need to 'low it, proper fights, I'm seeing her swing for people the way she used to swing for me, but listen, what am I saying, fucking, yeah, boy, the last time I remember it was over milk with one of our neighbours, they ended up on the floor still scrapping, pulling hair and scratching and all that, my mum licking the other woman with the base of his fist, her bones must's come weak, but still, my mum would never use certain words or insults. It takes a lot. But let me even try and give her a hug and her tongue will move mad.

67

XIII

Kwesi, come.

She unfolds the blue landscape, pressing down the ridges that rise from the creases, waiting for her son to find his way beside her.

See my house?

He follows the many white lines scrawling themselves into coherence, bending, curving, meeting again and crossing his impression. Staring for too long feels like the clashing lines took root in the grooves of his frontal lobe, so he closes his eyes and turns to look up at his mother.

Kwesi, see, this is your room. This is Maama's. This is where we'll do the garden.

He listens without opening up, under-standing his future ripple as his mother's finger passes over the page, rustling the compound, a test to insure . . .

Or you like this one to be your room?

These, the most words spoken at the thought of settling, laid out so she can finally rest.

It's not for me, Kwesi, it's for you. When you take holiday at least you have somewhere to stay. You don't have to ask anybody.

He wants to tear off a piece and place it in his pocket, show it to her when she can't part her lips, when deserting stone crumbles down a body too stiff to lift.

You like it? We've done well. Ay, Yesu, ma brɛ oo.

The boy watches the draft folding, detour ending, unable to recall a place for his mother. He wants to reach out, tell her to stop, open up again. Where will you stay, he wants to ask. Where do I look for you?

XIV

He used to touch her forged fibres,
    clench distant strands,
    and try to plait one side of her hair with
the other.
    Some days he'd hold on to the mesh,
    move it back and forward.
    Laugh, and she'd laugh too.
    Too many months since her last appoint-
ment,
    a few weeks left of this,
    and each morning she'd move it into
place,
    place her son in front of her and ask
how aligned it was.
    *Heh, wo sere?**
    He was the help to get it right before
work or church.

* My mum had one of
them laughs that the
harder it goes, the more it
starts to sound like that
cartoon character. That
duck one who never wore
trousers. Actually, that's
jokes because my mum
was the opposite. Ghanaian
mums don't see breasts
like the rest of the world,
it's mad. Bruv, obviously
I'm not talking about my
mum's breasts. Low it.

71

Sometimes, as she sat watching impaired yellow vans and drinks ordered in broken French, her son — heir to the flogging mischief before him — would stand behind her on the sofa, hands in her plastic, trying to lift.

*Kwesi, gyae,** I'm trying to listen.*

Then sitting, he'd look up at his mum and amuse his own hair, a deep touch, rising, pulling apart a tangle.

* I didn't even think my mum saw me as a child. Just because of the way she would move with me sometimes. But lemme not lie, I was a bit naughty, and she'd always give me a warning first, like a strong side eye or tell me to stop with a tone you just knew had violence on standby ready to come for you.

XV

'You like this one?'

He is okay. Ah, let him pass. Heh, I don't want trouble; go and clean your own area.

'What about this one?'

Eii, Awurade, this one has climbed from my bed before.

He had risen twice. But she would not return, she said, *don't touch me* she cried after he disgraced her the first time, swore to her father's feet, he could enjoy the smell of his own village without making his way to her olfactory. But he showed up and she gave in, convinced by the passion of his Kouros overpowering her Arden, *εyε hwam*, she would say,★ *me nim*,† he would say, but soon, they would travel

★ If I knew I was going out and my mum was cooking, I'd stay upstairs for like an hour while she did her thing, just sitting in my boxers with my garms on the bed, or I'd stand by an open window just in case. Soon as my cab arrived, I'd quickly put my things on, run down the stairs, shout goodbye to my mum, but she'd quickly come out, always clocking my steps from upstairs, she'd catch one whiff of my perfume and shout, asking me where I got it from. But I was gone! I doubt she ever heard me tell her I'd chat to her later. I'm surprised she even picked up on the smell, to be honest, because a few more seconds downstairs and no one else would smell it on me either. Can't be at a function smelling like Maggi, bro, c'mon.

† Man can't be arrogant and self-aware at the same time; feel sorry for people like that. I just thought of it now. Why? Yeah, sometimes I just switch up the vocab, get me. I'm like my man over there, acting like he's working.

73

again, and he would take his leave, always thinking ahead to come and go once more.

XVI

His finger can only clip the ridges of the
left spool as he begins again, begins another
run towards a taped wedding.

Tracking lines split a family gathered to
raise white cloths without the linked wings
of birds to ascend, supposed love still abroad
while the family dances on their union.
She tells her son –

'That's how we do it in our culture.'

Removed from the ceremony, she watches
too, her melding shelving without fear of
collapse.

Sat before the screen, aware of an absence,
is how her son knows he was there, once.

When is he coming, he sometimes asks.
'When is who coming?' his mother will reply.

XVII

Orange blossom clasps as it falls, pallid,
how could you tell as she lies in bed unable
to move anything but her hanging wrist,
fragrant and exposed, because moments
ago she rose ready for work, shimmying
through the Red Door, and now waves in
her son who peeks through the crystalline
panels, his wanting hands pushing forward,
slowly, nervous breaths expanding and
dissolving on the glass.

He puts his hands beneath her body and
tries to lift, roll, uses his head as leverage,
grinds his teeth, groans to summon who
his mum had promised tapped His foot
and thrown His strength along with His
image. God, flesh moves but nothing

significant, he slips his hands from under her, the numbness intimating something he cannot get free. The digital clock flashes and he knows she's late. Before now his eyes would have opened, twitching to acknowledge the boom and timid drop as the front door knocks. 'Is it happening again, Mum?' he finally asks. Fluttering, she flicks her wrist upwards to bring her son closer again but he hesitates, sliding a foot behind the other, bringing up dust on the surface not forgotten, distance recalling how much it hurt the last time.

XVIII

Her son pulls himself away from one hand, the other busy spooning enough Vaseline for him to finally slide into glory, calm until the late, nasal Gospel offering from the Ghana station begins playing on the clock radio flashing red for the last time of the night, they hope, tight, she grabs hold of her son's arm, digs nails in as she pulls him out of the house and into the lift, grounded when they reach the car meant to carry them through to the all-night church service, though now accounting for the auntie with the shine beneath her nose robbing a place, suggesting there's no space for two. Will even one speak up, will one disagree?

Then a cold breeze lifts their black and white ntuma* so those standing slide

* You know what else I'd say was trauma for man? Church, fam. My mum was always the one catching the spirit. It got to the point where I had to ask her if it was a set-up ting, was pastor calling her before church, telling her how to move when she got there. Because why was it always her? Sometimes she'd drag us to all-night services too. Even when my sister was a baby, she didn't care. God came first. Eight hours of praying and everyone looking at me when my mum went nuts or my sister started crying. Embarrassing. I used to be sooo vex. You know I've deeped it, my mum's clothes were always dark like they wear at funerals and everyone else's were bright with loads of colours, so the pastor would always know where she was and where to throw his prayer power. Proper hated those times.

back in, apologise, God will bless you, as they reverse, winter ice as such they can let go of the wheel, for a second, then leave the mother and her son still standing before the stretching faults they hoped to escape from, for one night, under God's arm or an anointed Peugeot roof.

* * *

It's okay, son, bring me my Bible.

She covers him, opening the Good News on a random page and reciting together with a finger under each line, mumbled words entangled with the confidence that sewn hearts will be spared on the last day.

XIX

These are who He smiles upon —
  wells when they leave His home but
remains solemn inside.
  A return, a renewal, a rebirth
  Sympathy cracks so empathy thrives.
  She stops the buggy at the bus stop and
faces her baby,
  pushes out her tongue
  playfully, acting, hoping, clopping her
lips around it,
  struggling to cross her eyes,
  but hears a forgiving giggle as the reply.

XX

There are no hums this morning, her mood pulling a vacuum out of jagged notes – like dust, thrown into the air by passing cars, mopeds, barking dogs throwing the chorus to others, bipeds, up and down the road trying to settle a back and forth that started indoors. None of her thoughts reach for a casual comment on her environment, she just sits, places her scalding cup on the centre table and leans back, the prey of the world waiting to be taken.

He saw it all, could tell she failed to feel from months before, no shock, no reaction as he watched plantain oil pop onto her skin to ward her off drowning it any further.

Again, she's severed a body part, abandoning it, another register, the call from the waif a floor above, the Moses basket could be teetering on the top step.

She looks up into a bulb that slowly bloats the eye so the mind can stretch, then blinks, forgetting her way to sleep; it's cheap, the bulb, each pound expanding its beam; each pound presses, moulding the plastic where she sits.

Listen.

'Mum?'

She's not moved; if she sits up, head forward, her hair will not follow, stiff, there's no use, her eyes out the window through curtains and patterned lining, onto the street where her son likes to play, where she'd wait, uncomfortable with his arrival but pleased he'd crossed the threshold.

XXI

Something shared, even agony, should
bring relief, so the boy looks into the new
eyes only just deprived of the many that
sing to His seat, and wonders why his old
tortures can't be re-enacted.

He finds her arm, pinches to wake her but
she is unmoved, breathes without ripples,
so he pulls his fingers back further so nails
grasp the skin.

Cries interrupted by a hiccup, too frequently
to allow consistency to the squall, so eventually, she gives up, as he does, eyes
searching for the cause, waiting for the
sudden impress on her chest, fascinated.

He waits with his sister, his own snatched breath after hers, his stifled laugh almost in time. He wonders when she will harden like him, thinks of her crown, soft to the touch, his mum always says, imagines her tiny lungs, so he pulls on a thread from the rising and falling blanket that covers her, and places it carefully on the top of her head. She closes her eyes again as he rubs the place where his nails almost broke the skin.

XXII

A lightning-shocked leather sofa against a blue painted wall decorated with scattered and filthy clothes along the top of the couch. Mother, leaning back, looking above, a head rest, corduroy bottoms and shirts, most unbranded, though one Ben Sherman purchased for her son to fit in at a neighbourhood party, the rest almost blending. She calls her son, who appears naked, no, in underwear, first of a three pack on the third day, tells him to speak to Maama, 'yes, it's my mum, Grandma,' she says, 'say hello, say it in Twi.' 'Haaalloo,' he shouts into the phone. *Eiiii, Twi na wo ka! My son, how are you?** He hands the phone back. For her, a smile to lead his departure, for him, a

* For some reason, and I've never understood this, the girls of my generation, the ones born here, they're always able to speak Twi better than the boys. Or they learn it faster. Tell me why? Is it because the girls spend more time around their mums? But then, Ghanaian boys are mummy's boys so how does that even make sense? My mum used to say it's because Ghanaian girls are too fast; not learning fast but a next kinda meaning. 'So that means you're fast too then,' I said to her. Hear her: 'Me? You're calling me fass? My friend be careful. I'm not your class-mate.' Classic. Yeah, alright then, Mum.

87

frown his path, brows close as he probes
the enthusiasm for a family that deserted
his mother's brittle bough.

XXIII

Anger masks tears for a mother's failing
frailty.

Her brother agrees and walks over to
who it was talking shit.

She points to the one whose words she
holds in her hands.

The accused shakes his head, rattled, to
repeat what was said about a mother's attire,

backwards, through his crunched collar.

'I wasn't the only one who laughed,' he
says between dodging crosses and being
choked by a closing fist.

'Say it again, you pussy,' he's asked. The
sister, looking her sibling up and down,
folds fear into inspiration – favour and her
brother's arm tightening, slowly rising

through the air. She screws her face, clenching and crushing those words and laughs, stands next to her brother and shouts, 'Yeah, say it again, you pussy.'

XXIV

Tea, tinned milk of course, one knife cavity more generous than the other, so she'll pour from that side while squeezing the top, of course, more drips to sweeten the tongue.

Next, she presses her thumb through the labelled packaging, *hmm, me kuromfɔɔ,** ignoring the peal, splits the plastic close to the top, pulls out the sweet dough and cuts into it, the knife compressing the thickness before splitting the loaf, the bakery's skilled knead making it softer than margarine, margarine she mixes with jam, the same knife to cut and spread, the piece thicker than if it were pounded and rounded, fool to diabetes, she sips tea that should scald but she is how old?

* Being an immigrant is stress. It's like once you leave Ghana part of your culture is stripped away or something. Like, you're always remembering your people instead of feeling like they're in your circle. Sometimes she just ain't with them. It's a weird one but it always seems like a reunion when my mum recognises something from Ghana. Well, more Kumasi than Ghana itself.

She bites and chews with mouth sliding to one side, another slurp to brown and drown, salivating while swallowing, no struggle going down
– the best of sweet bread feels like chewing on a cloud.

'You're invited,' she says to the children; they close in, but shake their heads in apology, so she enjoys alone, carries on chewing, brewing, diluting, consuming 'Ghana' bread, plus offering.

XXV

Brown envelope, split
  money will sometimes appear
  though her rebate dismissed

Who is there, Kwesi?
  Okay, bring them to me,
  Ah, saa brown letters, what do these people
want me to do?
  Son, put them under the table, ei, ma brε
ooo, I wish I have strength.

XXVI

If you want this style, be still.

Knees the vice touching widening ears but as yet not broad enough *listen*, lining up to a small TV for some leisure with intervals of a comb splitting head.

Parted, though tight inlet's constant pull will always swell and affect the landscape — *I said sit still, ah!*

Smells of green and blue falling, touching timidly, becoming the thought, the single strand of hair oiled to reflect whoever looks.

Then, she bends over, hands separating the mane, stretched puffs, breath wetting the cheek she leans in to kiss. *You okay, dalin? I'll finish soon, okay?*

'Mum, when can I do your hair for you?'

So, one plait reached up, and another with a broken tail presenting to disdain the process, globules of oil like obsidians on the surface of something appearing static, the architect now a child pulling 4C apart – left, right,

heh, don't pull too much,

'I'm not,'

her thoughts and fingers switching containers of green and blue, an intense red, mixed to the unruly, the passing images of tortured facial features guiding her grip and momentum, her will, powered by a heart severed of attachment.

The boy sitting opposite has rolled on his back, trying not to let one out because he must keep his mother sitting, hair twisting, fine fingers between three strands without a care for the direction or shape, she looks at the nape and slides two fingers over the baby hair she recalls being forced to endure. She pinches, her mother's head jerks but waits, ready to turn and return, riposte but who was playing? *Heh!* Her girl pulls the small hair again, hard, tight, front teeth pressed, you bitch, then is up before the boy can contain his bloated belly, starving, but here, content, flexing, nostrils flared, air tumbling out both ends, his mother's foot sliding on the settee cushion placed beneath her for saloon, her daughter already locked in the bathroom before she can find her footing.

XXVII

In the bathroom she sits so long, nothing
to dry.
    She should oblige.
    Drops, drown, torn.
    Runnels form, a daughter reborn after
passing.
    No sound of breath.
    How.
    My Lord.
    Mi ne sika★
    Awurade.
    She hangs up.
    Cries, tranquil heaves:
    expelled peace.
    Travel for waters to compete.
    He sneaks closer to the door.
    Mum?

★ I used to think Mum
was always lying about ps.
But then I opened one of
her letters by mistake and
I clocked it's not even a
joke. I don't even say
nothing when I give her
money. Imagine what it
was like back in the day
when she wasn't even
getting benefits. Or when
she didn't have me and
my sister. Mad. She's really
done her ting, though.

Kwesi?

What's wrong?

Kwesi, bring me tissue.

He used it all and forgot; but she feels the onus on her.

Sorry, he says.

He picks a loose roll from the black bag in the kitchen.

Are you okay, Mum?

Mmm, Kwesi. I'm fine.

What happened? he asks.

Nothing, Kwesi. Ghana. Mi bɛ ko Ghana. *I have to go there.*

She sneezes into toilet roll.

And her son wonders – why, why nothing syphoned from his mother's body is for herself.

* Always giving my mum ps is probably why I haven't been Ghana yet. I was supposed to go in like 2015 but that's when my granddad died and I was hearing it was a bit dangerous because they were splitting up his assets. Apparently some of the fam were banging juj too.

XXVIII

The numbers mean very little to her and seem smaller to the receptionist who asks her to step down, put her shoes on and sit again with the waiting maladies, patience, most unseen but some bouncing on knees, a fist to a cough or a build-up between brows as another is called in after sitting down while many are already adjusting to the roaming dust.

Her seat now taken, she stands against the wall, upper teeth set, daring her to talk. Korɔmfoɔ.* She rolls her eyes against the teef – cadaverous, legs crossed, posture disdaining the corrective attempts of the plastic seats, proud, *but she's sick like me so what's all this for?* A child's marbles rolling around the room, she turns to a post, a

* But to be fair, I owe my mum a lot. Like, a lot of money. Not because she looked after me, but because I used to teef bare. I don't even think she noticed because she never said anything. Or maybe that's why she was always vex. Rah, you know what . . .

double M to follow R, her hand glides above her scar, fighting to recall which of her children . . .

Then, a call from the heavy set in her ways makes bushmeat of her name, though good timing, as her thoughts were beginning to dissolve. In his office, where her eyes won't rise to the plaque with his name, gold yielding to his title, a mix of letters, if she tried they would finally find a place she can read, revealing a weak polished copper embossed with a familiar label, some shine, not much, so light, again? he asks. Okay, she says. All he can do is prescribe her the same, he says; she says, yes, she'll take it every day.

A signature and tear for codeine, she's sure it's in her head, where the pain has been, then she leaves without announcing another is to walk along the same dull pattern. She picks up Balmosa along with prescription; takes two pills and a palm of cream, rubbing her forehead, hoping this combined will cure her affliction.

XXIX

A woven crown, prickling circlet,

Anointing falling through, failing to spread,

Zealous tears of oil pull on strand of a neglected wig,

His palm slides, presses the centre of her scalp,

Thumb and a little finger able to stroke her temple

As he prays for her deliverance,

nkwan* staining her personal sermon,

Every word taking her back to repulsion.

But will God bless her if she doesn't stumble away from what she's seen?

* Listen, with Ghanaians, it's impossible to tell when they love you. With parents I mean. Mostly. But one day I just stopped thinking why is she here and started thinking, how long will she be here? Not in a badmind way. But yeah, then things started to shift. And I started clocking certain things. I noticed how when she dished my dad his food, she'd tell him there wasn't any more ties left in the soup, but then as soon as he went upstairs and I could eat (I never really ate around him. Dunno why. Just made me uncomfortable) I'd notice a fat one in my fufu. I remember the first time, I looked at her but she just blinked at me hard like to say, just shut your mouth and eat. Small things like that is how you know. Well, how I know. She does things in her own way, I guess.

XXX

Music, merge; banku, nimbus-like, drifting down swollen throats, taste secondary as halting voices try to align with buoyant word, catch every note, a party of few alive with the Ashanti soul. An auntie stepping off her stool, into the centre, 'hwɛ mi, hwɛ mi'* gyrating to the floor as Linda's name rings out, any woman is melodic, an instrument to the heartbeat of a West African man. She's low, hovering just above the floor, still moving her big bum back and forth to hip-life, stretching her arm up and saying 'okay okay, pick me,' eiiiiii, they scream, pitch in unison, claps to catch laughter, mouths raised to expel and catch their wails, a raining caterwaul, compelling sounds causing the singing from the system

* But obviously there were other sides. Like, I don't even know why, yeah, but whenever I was getting licks from my dad, my mum would just stare at me, never saving man. You know when you can just tell they hate you for no reason. Mad, boy. When I'd start crying or turn my face away, she'd just leave the room. No idea why she moved like that because I wasn't even that bad. To be fair, I noticed she never looked at my dad while he was doing all that as well.

to seemingly withdraw then pitch itself further in, weaving and rising with the harmony of the room to undulate like smoke across the ceiling. Through the dissonance, she is pulled to her feet, helped to stand by many including one she used to look down upon, the one who didn't look away or laugh as she rose, the one keeping time with the snap of her joints. They recognise the moment, their weak glares become stares above half smiles, the occasion becoming whole, feeling that the instruments and bones of the coast can bring even angels and demons together to dance.

XXXI

Her bleached palm circles clockwise, swift,
trying to wipe clean who or what came
before,

Days contain cavities, vacant hellos,
concern, breaking within the haste of time,

Years forge, dip and fold, preserved
calluses building under her cloth – blem-
ishes should be relished before she steps
to the table,

Again and again,

Day after day,

Face unmoving, belied when measured,
pace, time, gyina hɔ,* please,

Survey, decades as they pass, till you can
peer into her sky,

And see the forming pressure soon
collapsing on both of her eyes.

* Those were moments
when I'd think rah, this
woman really hates man.
Like, what did I actually
do. I think I even felt
suicidal. I don't even want
to use that word but
couple times while waiting
to cross the road, I'd think
about running into it, but
my mum would pull me
back, even though I
haven't moved, like she
could sense it, and say,
stand still.

XXI

XXXII

Kwesi, you know what happened to me today. You know my supervisor? Mark, the one who comes to pick me sometimes. Yes. I was standing near the lift. I was coming to sign in when he came behind me and he told me I was moving too slow for him. I said, ah, Mark, is it not you who told me I should start at four and it's now three forty-five. It's even early. He said, oooo, yaa, I mean you and me should move faster. I make my face like this and said, nonsense. I'm telling you, I told him, you know I don't tolerate such things. If he wants to work with me, he can come and work with me, but to be coming and telling me I'm working too slow and he too is slow, is it my fault? So we should move fast? I just climbed in the lift mcheew. These people, Kwesi, they're sick.

'Mum, why you always beefing someone.'

It's not me, Kwesi, it them who are causing me troubles.

XXXIII

The hands you'd like to console will impress, almost absorbed in rolling stress, a stance, swallowed to the wrist with how soft the body and tender the walk is, the look and half smile, arch of the lips, touching meekness.

A buckle comes loose, right, but once she reaches home children will be flittering through sleep, too weak to apply the balm of Deep Heat so she ignores the flailing gesture, the clipping rhymes for the attention of the street, and carries on to the Civic Centre.

Good afternoon from the corner of a lift and a how are you without a turn, bell, sidestep to let her get on with it. Have a good day. Oh, thank you, you too through a closing door and fading body, compressed as the elevation is secured, her potential ascent her supervisor can consider, one day, plus order more toilet rolls and gloves without the powder. *Sometimes it will be on my clothes and it's stucked so I have to get on the bus like that.* She sucks her teeth without a sound so blows her gum into her palm to better boil her spittle with frustration, mchew, extra returning to her mouth, then picks up her half-full caddy, looking forward to a back and forth.

She walks to her first class with buckle clasp still singing weak odes to school-time bells, turns to open the peeling, stickered and nail-scratched door, then, stops . . . watching shadows behind the square panel, an outline of obscured body and shade, how many had forgotten to leave – misshapes, mistakes, she slowly pushes through.

But – there were many of them, all waiting, all hollering, but why are they shouting? Happy Birthday! Are you surprised! *Me? It's* my *birthday?* She thinks, presents a tea-stained smile and Konkor cheeks. *Ah, me birthday, hmm* she hums, questioning dates and interrogating a page that brought her to 'life'. *Anyway, thank you*, she says, *mɛ dase,** she demurs. *Heh, Ismail, so you're here, I've caught you, where are the new gloves? Manager, my foot. Mchew.*

* But you know what, aside from all that, I give thanks to my mum, because, obviously, man can see it now, more clearly even, it wasn't easy for her. And lemme not lie, she weren't getting onto all the time. Sometimes she even moved like she *wanted* to be my classmate.

XXXIV

Kwesi, eh yɛ hwan*? P. Diddy?

. . .

You think I don't know things. I know.

Okay, Mum.

I know it's P. Diddy. Saa Jennifer whan whan. Was she not married to him?

Something like that.

Something like that. It's up to you. P. Diddy. Hmph, hwe ne ɛse.

Mum, man, I can't hear.

I'm just chatting with you and you're doing 'Mum, man'. If I fall down here you people wun't even care.

Oh my fucking days, Mum, please allow it.

Allow what? It's true, you don't respect me.

* Just so she could relate to me, or seem like she was down (she was always down to be honest, very calm, but calm people never see that they're calm – and that's even what makes them more calm), my mum always tried to remember the names of celebrities. I came home from school one time and she was complaining about a singer, saying there was too much 'should I, would I, could I' in one of their songs. That became her thing – whenever I would put on MTV Base, she'd say, not that song, like say she knew others on the channel. Like I could even choose. But when I just left it, she'd be quiet, looking at me now and then. I know she loved chilling with me.

115

You see me as this small woman. But when I'm gone, what will you do?

Aight, I'm going to bed.

Oh, my son. Don't be upset. Goodnight, anyway.

As he stands up she reaches out resting her hand on his bum.

Ayy, look at his bum.

Son, she calls, before he closes the door. He prefers son to any other calling, loves the drop of tone through those three letters, sounding stretched but comfortable in their balance, a name he's proud of, a lustrous designation so small but brilliant, a reaction of love touching his entire body when his mother summons him with such a small word capable of palpitating all the air around him.

He forgets annoyance, every anger an act when love struggles to escape.

Yes, Mum.

Make sure you off your light. Last night I had to come and close it for you. You know it's only me paying electricity, if you like try and pay.

Night, Mum.

XXXV

Her hand rubs her spine
  A son steps foot on her back
  Relief through labour

You okay, Mum?
  My back.
  You want me to walk on it?
  Mmm
  Okay.

CUSTOMS AND IMMIGRATION

I

'Do you remember when Mum used to stand in the front garden at night?'

*

A child's fear extends beyond their imagination so in the fringes of their fright lies the disquiet that touches them without their knowing. A little boy looks out the window at his mother, holding his eyes open for as long as he can to get used to the dark, so her silhouette is more pronounced and nothing issues from his mouth. He has turned off the TV but still, drawn images of killers may take shape behind him so he looks over his shoulder, then back at his mother, competing images somehow unreal but tangible. Her long night robe displays a descended black mould climbing the material, dragged across the floor to match dingy eyes that embrace Stygian sights. Then she moves, inward, duty bringing her back with the little girl, a baby who'll be thankful not to remember the intrusive fingers always pressing her fontanelle. The boy is told to take another bath as the close of day clings to his skin; he listens to the kettle wobble on its power source, watches the water bursting over the sides, and then there's nothing, sound or light, as the key depletes and everything is touched by the dark.

*

'Yes, I do, you know I do, you literally ask me this every time I see you.'

'Just saying, it was weird.'

II

This isn't it, though — he thinks of who
should be the one to care for her.

Norm-switching form and a Union Jack
sways outside the home she'll die in.

Does she know who he is, does she not
care or has the atrophy made her unaware,
who is there, a few drops left of memory.

He can't take it, her, what is this, Ghanaian
or not she planted her seed to bloom over
here, wafts of western idiosyncrasies
pungent to her frail identity.

On Sundays her hand slips into his, a light
renewal of platonic perfection, until her

son becomes someone else's reflection, the face of so many she loved but could never tell, though she always shows warmth to whoever approaches her church.

To watch a mother become a woman, deteriorate to become a girl, an infant who can't be held, waiting, unaware, to submerge with a family's final and stifled breath.

This is where she should be. Briefly, to see him smile she'll remember it was him, and she'll stretch her arms, an embrace with no charm, ingratiated with this terra, hell, an immigrant mother who will die here alone and can only rise with the body of work her son has done well.

III

The rising glare distorts the art thrown
onto the pavement – gum, spit, piss and
drink abstracting the day. He finally looks
up, surveys all he dismissed, picking up the
sound of hatching or the crunch of shells
when he strains an ear.

He sighs at an aunt's lack of vision, eyes
disappearing behind shoulders and heads,
bus stops and sign posts, hiding all but her
flushed demeanour and trembling fingers,
resenting proximity to the family and the
familiar. He watches her confidence climb
with each inanimate and stranger disguise,
but the oversight of her glances speak;
Auntie, you've learnt to walk on these
British streets.

Fading in, she pronounces, exclaims, raised octaves to hide her shame.

'My son!!!!!!! How are you, long time, how is Mum?'

IV

Night is made easy with drink, drenched, searching beams spiking into the space untouched by street lights, missing a body unbalanced, teetering between sobriety and something sombre. He is not depressed, but flat, a warm drip and spill on the top of his hand as he pushes himself to his feet, wipes his mouth and questions the distance between here and home. Whose home? But as one step follows another your eyes lean on a mother pulling a child from behind to walk by her side, then thrusting them forward to watch their pace before them. The child moans a little but you can see they enjoy leading the way, the inception of a skip, understanding who follows without looking back, feet tapping on the pavement, reverberating the way — yes, he'll see her again, but when he does, what is there to say?

V

He's always wanted to ask what she hoped
to achieve, 'without me', without displace-
ment, without history, a sentence without
words to follow, a life without a plot. She'd
say, she'd make life, what that means, he's
never known, looking back, what she sees,
he needs to let go, let her be. But . . . he
sees her, sees a desk, her fingers clicking
with a language partially known, but
writing for those who do, clarity, they say
they love her straightforward style without
embellishments, she is grateful, likes her
place, lifts her bottom from the swivelling
desk chair, presses the button and lets the
pressure raise it up, until her heels just
graze the carpet, a spin that pins down
exactly where her mind is, just outside her

manager's room, the CEO, closer to success,
or diminishing, simplified, this is her life,
the watered-down dream of a woman who
never understood what it meant to take
flight, that two lives can collide without
their soil being on either side.

VI

Can you spray some on the wrapping
paper, please?

Before he can pull the gift from the yellow
bag she tells him not to be like her, *to keep
your money, Kwesi, buying buying, you should
save.*

Escaping her craving for the thrall of
nostalgia, she tries to let herself settle in
the present, attention almost lost once more
when she catches the gifted scent of the
floating Red Door.

For me? Kwesi? Oh, thank you, son. Kiss me.
She pushes out her cheek, sways her lips

away. *Mmm. Mmm. You know I used to wear this one when I first came over?*

She lifts the top and sprays, both of them moving their heads around the room to catch the unravelling aroma.

VII

Love you, Mum.
  Why?
  What'd you mean 'why'?
  No, I mean why are you saying that.
  Because I mean it.
  Oh, okay, yeah, me too.
  You too, what?
  Heh, Kwesi . . . you don't have something
to do?

VIII

Home. He wonders if it's on Spotify; he wonders what it signifies, this warmth towards a high life that saw him so low before, how the music has changed over time and resentment has decayed into nostalgia. He sits and scrolls. And it finds him. Nana Acheampong. He thumbs play and closes his eyes.

♪ ♪ ♪ ♪ Ei! ♪ ♪ ♪ ♪

♪ ♪ ♪ ♪ Oh ♪ ♪ ♪ ♪

♪ ♪ ♪ ♪ Ei! ♪ ♪ ♪ ♪

♪ ♪ ♪ ♪ Oh ♪ ♪ ♪ ♪

Kwesi, pass me that.

A few shards of pepper test the taste of the carpet as a dimpled pestle is raised in the air once more, forcing the nail into the back of the bookcase, its unfolded lean rear covering still not secure enough, the beating cutting into the always pleading voice of Acheampong, a disembodied embodiment of a Ghanaian held 'pls'.

Na anka ebeye.

Her son now tries. Don't spoil it, she tells him, holding her two fingers just below the head of the nail, without nerves. Interestingly only concerned with her son's disappointment if he misses.

Na anka ebeye den naa.

Both hands around the pestle, one eye taking aim, he sways, torso side to side to a doubled *hwɛ, hwɛ, so you can dance, my son, look at his bum! Eii! Kwesi, saaa?* He grins and carries the movement through, down into the nail, submerging it halfway. *Well done, son.* Her turn again. *You know, I used to go disco,* she says, *sa song eh mi dɛ paa.* *

* So yea, that's my mum. You know what, every time I chat about her like this, I rate her even more. Are you gonna get her to chat to you as well? Good luck, boy.

136

♪ ♪ ♪ ♪ Ei! ♪ ♪ ♪ ♪

♪ ♪ ♪ ♪ Oh ♪ ♪ ♪ ♪

♪ ♪ ♪ ♪ Ei! ♪ ♪ ♪ ♪

♪ ♪ ♪ ♪ Oh ♪ ♪ ♪ ♪

Some at an angle, many tops slanted, others almost through though most missing the wood, prepped to pierce pages should they arrive on any shelf. They stand their creation, step back, survey side by side. She, your mother, tickles his palm with her fingers, then taps his softly, like natural notes, euphony, softly, they meet at their fingertips, the mirrored feet of a running spider. Then wrapping her little finger around his. *See, Kwesi, we did well. Aren't you proud of yourself? Let's bring the other box. We'll do your one today too.*

EPILOGUE

A factless interview. Taking place on 1 May 2019. This interview was intended to be the basis of this book, to give me everything I needed to write and understand my mother's story, from her arrival in the UK, up until the present day. Here she is, sitting in the living room, on an 'authentic' leather sofa without the plastic, a 3D picture of Jesus on an invisible cross just above her right shoulder, and a wallwide mirror to her left. Directly above her is 'The Last Supper', surrounded by wallpaper with scratched patches that were supposed to protrude slightly, scraped off during my childhood tedium. There are speckles of white powder collected in cliques about the floor, this being the odour with which she hoped to impress whomever she thought was coming to interview her. Once she knew I'd be doing it, she mentioned the fragranced powder was running out and asked could I please get some more – and hoover before I go out.

So, I'm here with my mum to ask a few questions about life. So, first thing, straight into it, what was it like when you were on the plane coming over?

It's normal.

Laughs Could you go into a bit more detail? You'd never been on a plane before. Were you excited, scared, what?

Yeah.

Yeah?

Yeah, of course you'd be excited; you are going through.

Okay. So, before you came over, what did you think of England? What did you think it was going to be like?

I dunno. I didin't think of it as anytin.

You didn't think of it as anything?

No. But when I came, I saw that it's nice.

It was nice?

Mmmmm.

Do you remember the first thing you saw and thought, eii, I'm here in England, I have landed?

Everything is different from Kumasi so automatically . . .

Yeah, but what was the first thing you saw?

What first thing I saw? Is it not the airport?!

Giggles Noooo, I mean what was the first thing you saw and thought, okay, this is different?
    Silence
    She thinks
    The environment.

The environment?

Yes, the environment because what it looks like, everywhere is pavement. In Kumasi is a lot of sand. Do you understand?

Sand?

In Ghana not everything was pavement like here. Heh, don't do me rough.

Mum, I'm just asking, man. So, was it Kumasi or Jamasi you came from?

Heh, you're recording it?! I didn't come from any Jamasi. I've never stayed in Jamasi.

Laughs Okay, okay. So where were you staying and with who?

Hey, I don't want to talk about such things.

Mum, it doesn't matter, no one is going to . . .

No no no no no. Don't go there. Don't record. Ask a different one. Hey, delete the recording.

Laughs Mum, no one is going to see your answers if you don't want them to.

But someone can take your phone and listen.

Listen to what? Two voices chatting? They will not care. How will they know who it is?

You're calling me mum and your voice is coming there. What are you talking about. Akwesi. Please. Ask me another one.

Okay, okay. Let's go past that. So, you were happy when you came over?

Yes.

Where was the first place you went?

I'm not going to give that description.

I mean like the first area, Tottenham, Edmonton, Peckham, Brixton?

Brixton. I went to Brixton.

Did you have any family when you came over?

Don't go there. Let me go, I'm going.

★Gets up★

No no, Mum, I'm sorry. ★Laughs★ I'm recording only for me. You can see what I write and if you don't like it, I'll delete it. Please, sit down.

Kwesi, I don't like these questions.

Okay, if I ask something and you don't want to answer, just say 'Pass'. Okay?

Hmmmm.

Okay, so.

Hey, son, is it me you're using for this book? You're coming to sell me?

No! The book is already written. This is bonus stuff.

I don't care. This is your final question, man.

Ah, Mum, please, allow it. You said you don't mind.

So, why are you asking deep deep questions like that? Just ask nice ones; I don't want to sell my story.

Okay, okay. Let's talk about work. Were you excited about the first job you got here?

Yeah.

What was the job?

Factory.

Factory? Okay. And you were excited. Okay.

Yes.

How long were you working there?

No. Ah, are your immigration officer? Hey, Kwesi, move your phone from here.

Mum, please.
  Okay, pass.

Okay, fine. So, you won't tell me how long you were working there?
  Pass.

Okay cool. Was it easy for you to make friends here?
  Mmhmm.

So, it was easy?
  Yes.

When you came over, were there a lot of Ghanaians already here?
  Mmhmm.

Mum, c'mon, give me some more than that.
  Yes! I said yes. Of course!

Okay, so because there was a lot of you here, did you come together and say, we are Ghanaians, let's . . .
  No, no.

So, what was it like?

You just see the person. He is Ghanaian. It was nothing. That's all.

So, you didn't say, hello, where are you from in Ghana and stuff like that?

Heh.

Laughs What now!

Pass.

Mum, I'm just trying to . . .

I said pass.

But why! I'm not asking details about you. It's the community. That's what I'm interested in, the community.

Okay, people were friendly, but it's just me. I find it hard to socialise with people.

Okay. Me too.

Is it me you're coming to write about?

Mum, I've already told you, no.

So, what is this for?

It's just extra content for the book.

Extra? So, how are you going to put it?

I told you, I'll show you first and then if
you don't like something, I'll take it out.
Cool, okay, so, yes, I've got a good question.
When you first came over, was finding a
church one of the first things you did?

No.

How comes?

Because I could pray at home. I was praying
by myself. I did my church at home. It was some
years before I had a church. I was just commu-
nicating with my pastor.

How did you talk to him? Were there like
calling cards you'd get so you could call
Ghana.

Mmm. I don't think. Actually, no, I'm not
sure you know. I think we just had to use
the phone boot. You put your money in and
when it finishes it finishes. We didn't have
them phone cards. I don't think so. It was
only BT.

Okay cool. Aight, I'm going to ask this
question. Say pass if you want to.

Heh, No, I'm done. Don't come into my life
like that. Don't penetrate into my life.

Laughs Mum, why are you being so dramatic. Okay, I won't ask it. Erm, okay, another question. When you came over, did you feel relief or did you miss Ghana?

Yes, I miss.

So, you missed Ghana.

Son, I say pass.

Mum.

I said pass.

Alright. Three more questions. Please. Did you feel stressed while you were here? Like, at the beginning? Like days where you'd wake up and think, ah, what am I doing in this country, I wanna go home?

Okay, ask another one. Ask all three and I'll choose which one I will answer.

Noo, you're not going to trick me, mehn.

Laughs *Kwesi, please, just ask. I have to go to work.*

Okay, fine. I'll ask one more after you answer this one.

Fine.

So?

So, what?

The question I asked you.

I dunno. I dunno. Not happy, not sad. I dunno. I dunno how I should answer it. Let me think about this one. Go to the next one and we'll come back.

You sure?

Mmm, a kinda. Yeah, I was a bit sad. That's it.

Okay. I'll 'low you. Thank you, I won't ask any more. Thank you for your participation.

Good. Hey, Kwesi, let me see what you've written before you come and sell me.

Laughs Yes, Mum. Love you, Mum.

Oh, leave me.

TRANSLATIONS

The languages spoken by the protagonist are English and Twi. These translations are approximations and a lot of their meaning and changing connotations may be lost.

ACKNOWLEDGEMENTS

I would like to thank my incredible agent, Crystal Mahey-Morgan, for putting up with me and always believing in my work. I'd also like to thank Jason Morgan and the entire OWN IT! team for their support. Thank you Roshni Radia, Berthy and Efia for reading over my early drafts and giving constructive but confidence-building feedback. Thank you also Korkor, Kaleke, Efe and Nancy for your words of encouragement. And thank you Kobby Ben for checking my Twi! Love to my boys Nels Abbey, Elijah Lawal, Symeon Brown, Jason Okundaye and Courttia Newland and Benjamin Zephaniah for having my back and talking me up every time I lost confidence. And thank you Billie Dee for every word, thank you Lillie Cat for every cry when you saw me down, and thank you Khaleesi Cat for laying with me when I was struggling to get up.

And thank you, Mum, for being you and doing all you've done.